Shadows in

Green

Richard E. Dansky

Shadows in Green
Richard E. Dansky
Second Edition Copyright © Richard E. Dansky, 2023
Published by Yard Dog Press at Kindle

ISBN 978-1-945941-44-3
Shadows in Green

Yard Dog Press
710 W. Redbud Lane
Alma, AR 72921-7247

http://www.yarddogpress.com

Edited by Selina Rosen
Copy Editor Leonard R. Bishop
Technical Editor Lynn Rosen
Cover art by Angeline Shearstone

Second Edition, July 15, 2023
First Edition March 1, 2004
Printed in the United States of America
0 9 8 7 6 5 4 3 2

Dedication

For Jacob Benjamin, whose uncle will make sure to keep him out of the woods.

Shadows in Green

A smart Yankee boy should always know his place, and that place sure as hell isn't the South Carolina woods in the middle of the night. That's what I told myself afterwards, but afterwards isn't any good. It never is, not when it comes to things like that.

The whole mess started on what was euphemistically called a company retreat. I worked for a small publishing company in those days, a place called Damocles House that used words like "non-traditional" and "edgy" to cover up the fact that the people running the joint didn't have any damn idea of what they were doing. They'd heard just enough buzzwords to be dangerous, and that's how the entire company wound up hip-deep in the Carolina woods.

It was supposed to be a team-building exercise, which is marketing-speak for "everybody gets hammered together and bonds over puking in the same toilet bowl." The schedule called for personality tests and workshops in the morning, wacky sports competitions in the afternoon, and evenings full of beer, vodka and violent illness while the few single women we employed got dive-bombed by opportunistic suitors. The last wasn't on the *official* schedule, but frankly, it was the only set of activities anyone was liable to pay attention to.

Management's first mistake, of course, was coming up with the whole thing. Their second was the choice of location. They had rented out one of those southern "resort" complexes, all white-sided cabins in the middle of nowhere, that you find along the Carolina-Georgia border. There's a huge manmade lake there and not much else, except for a couple stores that sell fireworks and moon pies. As a result, the entire area is littered with that sort of joint, places with names like "Pine Grove Acres" where car dealers from Marietta can take their wives and kids off for a weekend in the "country." It's all very nice and sedate and white-bread, and that's why the muckety-mucks had rented out the entire place for us. It wasn't that there were that many of us; at our biggest, we never had more than a hundred people. No, it was that they were afraid one of the artists would hit on the wife of some minister from Cobb County and all hell would break loose.

We'd gone up on a hot and sunny Friday morning, the entire company caravanning along because the site's printed directions would have sent anyone who followed them a hundred miles deep into Alabama. A long line of cars, equal parts SUVs and Saturns, snaked its way up I-85. The conga line was slowed only by frequent breaks for stops for bathroom breaks, and lightning-fast runs into roadside liquor stores for "supplies". I drove, mainly because I didn't trust most of my coworkers' cars to get us there in one piece. Raises had been small that year, in part to pay for the misbegotten retreat, and as such most of the creative staff was operating on the "keep a roll of duct tape and a can of oil in the trunk" theory of auto maintenance.

The car was full for the trip up. I'd foolishly volunteered to play pack mule, so my noble little sedan had the burden of transporting three of my coworkers and their small mountain of stuff to the wilds of South Carolina. The entire trip up I drove with one eye on the rearview, half-expecting to see the trunk explode open and evacuate a potpourri of sleeping bags, black t-shirts and small, carefully sealed baggies full of grade-A Tallahassee-grown weed.

The latter belonged to one of the occupants of the back seat, an accountant named Harris Brahms. The office's serious stoner, he was in his mid-30s but liked to chase college women, and had a haircut that made him look like a roadie for Grand Funk Railroad. Harris came from a long line of law enforcement officers, and his stated goal was to someday go to work for the DEA. I'd made the mistake of asking him what job he thought he was qualified for with them, and he just smiled. "Easy, man," he'd said. "Tester."

Sitting next to him was Felix Gotti, who insisted on being called "The Cat." Felix was six foot two and balding, a horndog of the first water. He'd stumbled into a job as a line editor a few years back and clung to it with the ferocity of a man hanging onto a branch over a sleeping grizzly. He was from Georgia and spoke with a deep twang, something which was made much more amusing by his penchant for wearing colors that came right out of a post-volcanic sunset. If it wasn't orange, it wasn't stylish enough for Felix, and that was that. No one had yet figured out what was so particularly catlike about the man, but no one had been brave enough to ask him about it. Felix and Harris had diametrically opposed tastes in music, if not pharmaceuticals, and that was one of the reasons I'd stuck them in the back seat together.

And sitting in the front seat, as always, was Ellie. One of the copy editors, she looked like someone had ordered a feisty pixie from Central Casting. She was maybe five feet tall on a good day, a brunette with a pageboy haircut and a strong Laura Ashley tropism. Her face was dusted with freckles, her eyelashes were impossibly long, and her mouth made a man really want to be an oboe reed on the off chance she decided to take up playing woodwinds.

And needless to say, I had it for her, bad.

The trip took all of two hours, though the unpacking took longer. By the time everyone had settled into their bungalows—the four of us were tucked into one, with me sleeping on the couch to ensure Ellie a private bedroom—the day was pretty much shot. There was a half-hearted attempt at getting everyone together for an organizational meeting to discuss the next day's agenda, but attendance was pitiful. Hector, the company's CFO, tried to explain how the next few days were important for getting to know our coworkers, learning each others' personalities, and finding new ways to work together, but at the end of his spiel, the only question anyone had was "When's dinner?" Outside the main meeting room, you could hear the whooping and the shouting; the party had already started.

By sundown, things had gotten out of hand. People were hanging out of windows waving half-empty bottles, screaming and laughing like it was going out of style. A half-dozen stereos had been cranked, each with a different CD, turning the central area between the bungalows into the audio equivalent of the Somme. Somewhere nearby, glass was breaking as empties fired at a trashcan missed their mark.

I sat on the front step of our little cabin, nursed a Sam Adams, and shook my head. I didn't actually like drinking Sam, mind you, but it was from Boston, and as a recent transplant from New England I felt that I had to keep up appearances. "What a mess," I said to no one in particular, and took another drink.

"Agreed," Ellie replied from over my shoulder. "Got room for two on that step, Ben?"

"Sure," I said as enthusiastically as I dared, and wiggled over to the side a bit. She dropped down next to me, a can of Sprite in her hand, and tucked her legs up under her. "Some party," she commented, without enthusiasm.

I nodded, took a swig of beer, and turned to face her. "Not exactly my speed, I confess. I don't mind the occasional drink, but this..." My voice trailed off and I waved in the general direction of the idiocy. Forty feet away, two of the assistant editors were swinging broomsticks at each other in a miserable impersonation of a swordfight. I averted my eyes from the incipient carnage, and managed to wince only a little when I heard one of them yelp in pain.

"Yeah, this is just kind of stupid." Her voice was surprisingly fierce. "I'm not sure how it's supposed to make me work better with these guys because I've seen them fall over drunk into a rain barrel."

I chuckled. "That's the point, you see? The next time Noel or one of the other guys from content management comes down and bitches you out, just think about what they looked like out here, hanging from some tree by their underpants and trying to remember their own names. I guarantee you the conversation will be much more amusing after that. She laughed, and I grinned back at her.

"You're going to get me in trouble," she accused, but there was no heat to her words.

That's the idea, I nearly said, but bit back the words and instead put on my best innocent face. It didn't work, but it did send her into a whole new spasm of laughter.

"So," she said when her giggles finally subsided, "what else is there to do here?"

"Not much," I admitted. "You can get drunk with layout, get drunk with editing, get drunk with the finance department..."

"Or we could explore," she said firmly, and bounced to her feet.

"Explore?" I looked up at her quizzically. "Explore what?"

"Harris found something. It's neat." And with that, she vanished back into the cottage. I thought about not following her for all of six-tenths of a second, then got up and went inside.

Harris and The Cat were sitting around the living room coffee table when I meandered back, Cat and Ellie on the couch and Harris squatting on the floor. "What's up?" I asked the gathered assemblage.

"Harris had a great idea," Ellie announced breathlessly. "Why don't you tell him about it?"

"Sure thing." He blinked owlishly, then looked up at me. "Basically, the one thing all four of us have in common is that we don't really dig the party scene they've got going right now, right? I mean, you don't look like you're having fun, Ellie's got her face scrunched up like she just

5

swallowed a lemon every time she looks out the window, and Felix and I both prefer a more...relaxing sort of chemical recreation."

"Damn drunks are too damn loud," Felix chimed in, scowling.

I nodded in cautious agreement. Sad as it seemed, drinking was the social equalizer inside the company. If management hadn't seen you half-wasted and licking a fence post, you weren't their kind of people and they flat-out didn't trust you as a result. This meant that even if you weren't necessarily the biggest partier out there, you kept your mouth shut about your entertainment preferences lest you get labeled as having "the wrong attitude." Having the wrong attitude got people fired, demoted, or put on shitwork projects, and I wasn't particularly interested in any of those outcomes.

Harris, to his credit, didn't seem to notice my internal dissertation, and plowed right on. "Cool. So unless we want to hang around all night listening to those tools have fun, we need to find something else to do."

"But we're in the middle of nowhere, dumbass," The Cat interjected, his accent getting thicker as he got more animated. "There ain't a damn thing else to do around here, unless we want to get lost and then get sodomized by some hillbillies on a fishing trip." He held up his hands and mimed playing the banjo. Ellie hit him on the arm, hard. He winced and held up his hands in a gesture of surrender, and she flashed me a tiny victory grin. For that alone, I was ready to marry her.

"We don't need to go anywhere," Harris replied, unperturbed. "I was poking around the main office after I finished unpacking, and they have all these informational packets and maps and things. It turns out this whole place is built on an old plantation, and there's a lake around here somewhere, too."

"So what are you proposing?" I asked, warily. "A midnight swim? Or an amateur archaeology expedition?"

"Sort of," he admitted, and grinned. "Look, being around here is going to suck. It's going to suck a lot. So why don't we just all go for a walk and explore the place a little bit? You know, see if we can find the ruins of the house, find the lake in case we want to blow off the programming tomorrow and go for a swim, and just generally get away from the idiots." He turned to me, as if sensing my reluctance. "Don't be such a city boy, Ben. Don't be such a *Yankee.* Contrary to what you might believe, the woods are not full of gators, snakes and rednecks just waiting for their chance at your wallet and firm white ass. Hell, it's safer here than walking around oh-so-civilized Atlanta." As if to accentuate his words, a string of firecrackers went off outside. Screams and giggles followed, muted slightly by distance.

Cat shuddered. Ellie looked over at me. "What do you think?" she asked.

I chewed on my lower lip for a minute. Going off exploring with Ellie sounded just fine to me; going off exploring with Ellie and the boys considerably less so. "Well, it beats waiting for the fireworks to come in the front window," I muttered, mostly to myself.

"What?" Cat asked.

"Nothing." I set my beer down on the table. "Screw it. Let's go."

In actuality, it took us about an hour to get everyone vertical, fed and ready to roll. This was enough time for me to grab both another Sam and time to talk to Ellie. The former became necessary as I listened to Harris and Cat snipe back and forth at each other over where exactly we'd be exploring; the latter was just a happy accident.

"You sure you want to do this?" I asked her.

She nodded. "What else could we do tonight?"

A few answers ran through my head, but I stopped them before they got to my mouth. "Well, I was thinking that if you wanted to just go somewhere and talk, that would be fine, too. Less chance of stepping on a snake, for one thing."

She grinned, prettily, and I blushed. "That's very sweet," she said, and patted my cheek. "Maybe tomorrow night, OK?"

"OK," I said, even as she was walking off.

OK indeed, I thought, and watched her walk, in every sense of the term.

It was dark by the time we left the bungalow, the sort of dark you don't get back in the city. As we trooped out of the front door, armed with bug spray, one lonely flashlight and a vague idea of where we were going, I gaped up at how big the sky seemed. The lights on and in the bungalows seemed very small somehow—there was just a huge expanse of open sky, filled with stars and a fat, lazy moon peeking through the trees. Back home in Connecticut, you were lucky to get a couple dozen stars, even on the nights when the Hartford city lights didn't turn the sky dull purple. But here, the sky was something else, something huge.

"That's one hell of a view," I said, and pointed straight up with the flashlight. Harris nodded, while The Cat just whistled.

Ellie took my arm proprietarily and pulled me forward. "It'll get better when we get away from the buildings and the lights and the noise. Come on!"

We went, her enthusiasm tugging us all along in her wake. Moving up the paved driveway we walked, we took a turn onto the gravel road that had so thoroughly assaulted my sedan's undercarriage on the way in. Right would have taken us back toward the highway; we turned left, and went deeper into what we imagined would be our little magical mystery tour. Our footsteps crunched in lumpy syncopation as we stomped along, and within a couple of minutes, a bend in the road left the resort—and its lights—behind.

Ellie halted. "Now, look up," she said. Obediently, we stopped and did.

It was breathtaking. The slash of sky visible between the trees that lined the road was liberally spangled with stars, brighter and fiercer than any I'd ever seen before. For the first time in my life, I could see the pale band of the Milky Way. It was astonishing. Unencumbered by street lamps and fast-food marquees, the stars glowed aggressively down on us.

Harris whistled. The Cat nodded a few times and said something that was probably "Dang." Ellie stood there, face upturned so the stars could bathe it in their light, her expression a mask of rapturous glee.

And me? My attention was already slipping to something else.

Because on either side of that ribbon of sky were the trees, and they were not to be ignored.

That's not quite true, now that I think back on it. The trees themselves you could ignore, but the shapes they made in the night, those you couldn't tear your eyes away from. If you did, something would move in the corner of your sight and convince you the whole forest was just as interested in you as you were in it. There was reasonable evidence that trees were in there *somewhere*, looming over us from either side. *Something* had to be under that curtain of greenery, after all, something that grew straight and tall and threw out branches in every direction to hold it up. But the trees themselves were invisible; trunk, branch, and leaf. Every inch of forest was covered in leaves so thick they looked like snake scales, overlapping and hissing against each other in the evening quiet.

Ellie followed my eyes and nodded. "Kudzu," she said, and that was enough.

I nodded, and added a thoughtful "Hmm." I'd heard of kudzu, of course—some southern plant or other that grew fast and wrapped itself around whatever was handy—but I never imagined it like this. It smothered the trees from root to crown, giving them a new skin of hungry leaves. It was impossible to tell where one left off and the next began, so thick was the greenery between the trunks. And the branches—the branches were worst of all. Heavy with their parasitic load, they leaned out toward the road, dripping long lengths of vine.

Look at them just right, and the trees were no longer trees; they were hooded, misshapen figures lurching toward the road, the play of their branches' shadows evidence that they were reaching out for us. I found myself scanning the rows of smothered pine and sycamore for dark eyes looking out at us, waiting to hear the tell-tale creak of a splayed-root foot pulling free from the earth and lurching toward the road that dared cut its way through their domain.

"Spooky, isn't it?" Ellie said, and leaned in close. I pulled her in a little closer, and it didn't seem like she minded.

"You can say that again. What is this stuff again?"

"Kudzu," The Cat interjected, parking himself on Ellie's other side. "Amazing stuff, ain't it? Came over from Japan 'bout a hundred years ago, and now it's everywhere. Grows eighteen inches a day. Y'all can actually see it getting bigger as you watch. It's damn near impossible to kill, too. You pretty much have to burn it out, or anything it starts growing on is screwed."

"What happens to the trees once it starts growing?" I asked, and pointed to one particularly fearsome-looking specimen. It had no fewer than four branches extended over the road, each enrobed in vines and dipping dangerously low over our heads. Never before had I seen a tree that looked so ready to *pounce*.

"Shit, man, that's easy." Harris walked up, shaking his head. "It dies."

I looked around our little circle, and was unsurprised that we'd closed ranks against the night. I saw Ellie turning from left to right and realized she'd noticed the same thing, so I gave her a smile and looked up at the sky again.

Blinked.

Took a deep breath.

And told myself that it was just my imagination, and that the little strip of sky visible over the road had *not* gotten narrower in the last five minutes.

"...thing left."

"What?" I tore my eyes away from that thin slice of sky and focused on The Cat. He was nodding slowly, his hands moving animatedly as he expounded on the wonders of kudzu. He looked at me, annoyed I hadn't listened the first time but pleased he got to serve as an authority again. "Like I said, man, this here stuff is unbelievable. It grows up on a tree and the tree can't get any light. It just dies under there."

I waved my arms, pointing to everything in the vicinity. "So you're saying that all of those trees are dying?"

He grinned like a blissed-out Cheshire Cat. "Yup. Or dead. Just smooth gray wood and gnarly branches, like long fingers under there, and all of it starting to rot."

I shuddered. "Thanks so goddamned much for the image, man. Do we want to stay here? One of these things might be rotting enough to fall over on us."

"I think they make sure the ones near the road will stand up," Ellie offered, but she was the first to start off down the narrow strip of gravel and into the further dark. Harris and I looked at each other and then followed, leaving The Cat to bring up the rear.

After a good fifteen minutes' walking time, we found the first evidence of the old plantation: the remnants of a small house's foundation, stone mortared to stone in a square ten feet on a side. "Smokehouse, maybe?" I offered doubtfully as the flashlight beam played over it, a bare five feet from the side of the road.

"Maybe," Ellie said, unconvinced. "I wonder where the main house is."

"Back in there," I replied, gesturing toward the deeper woods. As I was still holding the flashlight, this caused the beam to dance crazily over the leaves. The kudzu had started making inroads here, too, and while the trees weren't entirely encased in the stuff, it looked to be only a matter of time.

Felix leaned in toward the woods, then shook his head. "No way. We are not going back in there at this hour of the night. All we need is to have someone fall down an old well or pop an ankle in a gopher hole because y'all couldn't wait until morning to go play in the dirt. The rocks will be there in the morning, guys, I promise."

"But it won't be as much fun in the morning," Ellie protested, only half jokingly.

I caught her eye and winked. "And besides, we have programming that we *have* to do in the morning. Now's our only free time."

"Free time, my ass," Felix grumbled. "You can go. I'm not wandering around in the woods in the pitch dark. Probably redneck cannibal zombies waiting back in there with their pet cottonmouths." Harris stood beside him, nodding agreement that was silent apart from the occasional "Yeah, man." Both looked grim.

I frowned, and started to feel my resolve slip a little bit. Going off into the woods at this hour wasn't exactly my idea of a brilliant notion either, but Ellie wanted to and Harris didn't, which meant that backing Ellie was a moral and hormonal necessity. Besides, I had the flashlight, and we were still within shouting distance of all our drunken coworkers in case there actually was some kind of emergency. Faced with such unassailable logic and moral conviction, common sense packed up its bags and left, leaving me standing there racking my brain for something witty to say.

To buy time, I played the flashlight's beam back and forth in the gap between the lowest tree branches and the ground. The light stabbed out into the woods and I waggled it a bit, hoping for a direction to emerge from the darkness.

At the edge of vision, one did. Or maybe it had been there all along, and I'd just missed it the first time I'd looked that way. Something that looked like stone and metal gleamed there in the light, just at the edge of vision. I squinted, trying to get a better look, and took a step toward it off the road.

"What are you looking at?" Ellie asked, hope in her voice.

"I'm not sure." I took another step off the gravel and raised the angle of the beam. More stone reared its head into the light. "I think I may have found the main house, though. There. Do you see it?"

She turned, triumphant, and jabbed Harris in the chest. "See? It's right there. We won't even be out of sight of the road. Come on." She grabbed his hand with both of hers and tugged.

He didn't move, instead shaking his hand free. "No way," he said stubbornly, and tucked his thumbs into his armpits. "I'm not going in there, not at night, anyhow."

"Fine." Ellie deliberately turned her back on him. "I'll be going alone, then, unless someone," - she gave me a pointed look—"wants to escort me with the flashlight and keep me safe?"

"I'd be honored," I said, and felt my face melt into a shit-eating grin. Harris saw it too, and his expression went as sour as year-old yogurt. "Why don't you and Felix stay here and wait, Harris, in case we get into any trouble. That sound good to you?"

"Yeah, whatever." He sounded equal parts disinterested and pissed off, but The Cat had already plopped down on the road cross-legged and pulled out a lighter. Looking down with disgust, he waved us into the woods. "Just don't take too long, OK? I still don't think it's safe out there."

"Five minutes," Ellie promised, and then dragged me under the trees.

It was quiet off the road, and dark. The sound of Harris' bitching faded within a few footsteps, and then it was the sound of our feet on the dried branches and dead leaves. A quick look up told me that no starlight or moonlight was making it through the canopy of leaves. It left us to wander by flashlight in what seemed more and more with every step like a sort of cave, one with stalactites of leafy vines and stalagmites of rotting tree stumps thrusting up from the mulch.

"Listen," I said, and stopped. Ellie did the same, then turned to me, puzzled.

"What is it?" she asked, her voice managing to echo off the trees.

I waved at her with my off hand. "Don't say anything. Just listen. What do you hear?"

She looked around for a moment, trying to understand my concern. "I don't hear anything."

"That's what I mean." I looked around nervously, then brought the flashlight around to illuminate her face. "Shouldn't there be insects or frogs or something making noise out here?"

"Well, there should be, yes." She looked briefly confused, then turned toward our destination. "The camp owners probably bug sprayed them out of existence," she said over her shoulder. She didn't sound terribly convinced, but she didn't stop, either, and pressed on into the dark. Holding the flashlight more tightly and looking down every time I stepped on something that crunched, I followed.

It wasn't the foundations of a house we'd seen. I realized that when we got close. Instead, it was a low, wrought iron fence half-gone to rust, and inside it, a double row of stones. "Jesus," I said when we were close enough to see what we were approaching, but Ellie's response was "Cool!" and she ran forward to check the little graveyard out.

There were eight upright stones set four and four; I saw when I joined her at the fence. Four more flat grave markers rested off a bit, in the corner of the plot. The stones were old, that much was certain—weather had eroded the names enough that they were unreadable by flashlight. The graveyard itself was perhaps twelve feet by twenty, mostly overgrown with weeds and brambles, and bounded by that rusty, waist-high fence. The tops of the fence poles, I noticed with relief, were rounded, which meant that Ellie wasn't liable to give herself tetanus by leaning over them the way she was. There was a gate, which looked to have rusted shut, and something vaguely reminiscent of a path between the stones, but there was no other sign that this graveyard had been tended any time in the last ten years.

"Look," said Ellie, and pointed. "The little stones. They're all off in the corner. Must have been children who died."

I nodded. "I guess this was the family burial ground, though it's not very big. They must have lost the land pretty quickly."

"Probably after the Civil War," she agreed, and wandered off into what presumably was thought about the long-ago events that had transpired in that very place.

I stood there as she poked about for long minutes, looking at the gravestones one after the other. "We should go," I finally ventured, when it was clear that she'd seen about all there was to see.

"I guess so," Ellie replied absently. "I just wish I could see the names on the tombstones, so we could look the family up and see what happened to them."

I scanned the flashlight beam over the largest of the grave markers. It was red granite, unusual down here, and showed nothing more than the fact that carving had once adorned its face. "We're not going to see anything tonight. Maybe we should come back tomorrow, like Harris said."

"What, and miss the Myers-Briggs test?" For a moment I thought she was serious, and she laughed delightedly when she saw my expression. "Of course we'll come back tomorrow. I don't want to do any teambuilding exercises. I don't particularly want any of our coworkers on my team."

"Not any of them?"

"Well," and she smiled. "Maybe one. Let's go."

We got back to the road in short order and without incident. The entire way back, Ellie spun elaborate fantasies about what we'd seen and what might have happened here. She was ready to burst at the seams with things she wanted to tell our erstwhile partners in crime, whom she was convinced were bitterly regretting their decision to stay behind.

But when we schlepped through that last curtain of leaves, we got a nasty surprise. Harris and The Cat were gone.

"Fuckers!" I said, which I thought was quite reasonable under the circumstances.

"They probably just got bored," Ellie said in a soothing tone, though she wasn't able to keep the annoyance entirely out of her voice either. "I'm sure it's no big deal. Let's just go back to the resort and find out what happened."

I nodded, muttered something about the goddamned stoner freaks under my breath, and started trudging back up the hill toward the bungalows. Ellie walked with me, close by my side, and our footsteps synched up within a couple of paces. Somewhere off in the distance, a single cicada started its song, waited for its friends to join in, and then thought better of the whole idea.

Good call, little bug, I thought, and marched homeward in silence.

"*What the fuck* happened to you two?" I asked Harris and The Cat over breakfast the next morning, somehow keeping my voice just under a roar.

They exchanged guilty glances. Ellie and I exchanged quizzical ones as she took a bite of her English muffin, and then Harris said, "You tell them."

"Aww, crap." The Cat put his fork down in the middle of his scrambled eggs. "Y'all are not going to believe this, guys, but I swear it's true. We didn't want to go back, but after you went in there, things got...well, they just got plain weird."

"Weird," I echoed tonelessly.

"Weird," he repeated, and nodded with all the vigor he could muster at 8:30 AM. "Seriously weird-like. First of all, we should be pissed at you. Y'all said you were going in for five minutes, but you were gone for over an hour, with us sitting there getting more and more worried, and-"

"Wait a minute," I interrupted. "No way were we gone for an hour. That was a five-minute walk each way, and we spent maybe five minutes total in the graveyard."

"It was an *hour*, man," Felix insisted.

"You were stoned, Felix," I said through gritted teeth. "You think it takes half an hour to make minute rice when you've been smoking."

"No way. I was looking at my watch."

"In the dark?" I snorted.

He held it up for me to see. "It's got one of those light-up faces, asshole. And it was at least an hour, I swear. And when you stepped off the road, you guys just vanished into the woods."

"Now that's ridiculous." Ellie jumped in, full of righteous disapproval. "We were just off the road the whole time, and you should have seen the flashlight beam, even through the leaves."

"Should have, yeah." Now it was Harris' turn. "But you went in there and it was like the leaves just walled themselves up behind you. We couldn't see a thing. Couldn't hear you, either, though we tried yelling."

Ellie and I exchanged a worried look. "We didn't hear you at all," I said, more softly. "Are you sure you shouted?"

"Positive." Harris took his fork and jabbed in my direction with it. "Nice and loud, even. But that's not why we left, even if we did think you two were being pricks."

"Or screwing around," The Cat added. Ellie wadded up her napkin and threw it at him. She missed.

"We were not screwing around," she said firmly. "We walked in, looked at the graveyard, and walked out. It did not take us an hour, we didn't hear you calling, and I think you're both just lying."

They looked at each other again, clearly uncomfortable. When angry, Ellie was formidable in the way only small pretty women could be, and no man within her sphere of influence ever wanted to risk her wrath.

"There was one other thing," Harris reluctantly offered. "That's what really made us go. We would have waited otherwise, I swear."

"We were going to stay, honest," The Cat chimed in.

"Uh-huh," I said. "Do tell."

Harris swallowed nervously and fidgeted with his fork. "It was the trees."

"The trees?"

He swallowed, hard. "It looked like—and I know neither of you are going to believe this, but I swear it's the truth—it looked like they were moving."

"That's called wind, Harris," Ellie said icily.

"Not like that!" He took a deep breath and shuddered. Next to him, Felix wouldn't meet my eyes. "So help me God, they looked like they were leaning down towards us, and the branches were curving and moving against the wind, and then they started even edging closer to the side of the road-"

"Enough." I held up my hand in what I hoped was a commanding gesture. "You two have got to be kidding me.

18

You ran off and left us in the woods because you thought the trees were chasing you? What the hell were you smoking last night, anyway?"

"You don't hallucinate on weed," Harris said sullenly. "And I know what I saw. What we saw. You saw it too, didn't you, Felix?"

Felix stared intently into his own lap. "I think so," he said softly. "It was really dark."

"Great." I smiled cheerlessly. "Well, now that that's cleared up, why don't we move on. Ellie wanted to go back there during the daytime so we could get a look at the graveyard we found back in the woods."

"You found a graveyard?" Harris perked up a bit. "That's cool."

I nodded. "It is cool, and I promise you the trees will stand absolutely still during the daytime." I waggled my fingers at him menacingly. "They only come out at night, you know."

"Screw you," he said, but it was without heat. "So, what, you want to go back there?"

"After breakfast," Ellie nodded.

"Fuck breakfast," said Felix, and gave the scorched strips of bacon on his plate the hairy eyeball. "This stuff will kill you, man." As one, we rose and dumped our trays at the trash barrel, then headed for the door. Ellie bounced outside first, The Cat following.

Before we got outside, I grabbed Harris by the elbow and hauled him out of Ellie's earshot. He faced me, mouth set in a thin line. "Yes?" he asked, and fluttered his eyelashes.

"Look, I know it's none of my business," I said, "but do me a favor? No goofy bush today until we get back, OK?"

"You know not what you ask," he replied theatrically, then grinned. "No worries, bro. Don't need it during the day. But tonight, you just might want some."

"I don't think so," I said, and let him go.

The hike to the old plantation site took longer during the day, something that surprised me. Most of the walk was done without conversation, though Harris occasionally moaned about the fact that we hadn't found the lake. Only Ellie felt like talking, and she kept up a constant stream of commentary on plants, birds, and anything else we walked past.

"You know," she said to me softly at one point, "I can understand now what they saw last night when they were..." she mimed toking, and went on. "The trees really do look like figures under the kudzu." I nodded. In the daylight, the vegetative amoeba was less eerie, but more impressive. I could see now how thick the growth was, and how fast it scaled new trees. Dozens of yards of woods at a time were covered in broad, flat leaves, a landscape in living green. Even trees that I could have sworn were clear the night before were now part of the vast emerald carpet.

"They still left without us," I replied in something that wasn't quite a grumble.

"Well, yes, but that left us more time together. To talk," she added hurriedly, and then skipped off to point out to Felix some variant or other of the yellow-bellied sapsucker.

I grinned, and kept grinning all the way back to the spot where we'd dared enter the woods.

It wasn't hard to find. For one thing, the walk was ninety percent downhill, which made it a pleasant, fast stroll. For another, the detritus from The Cat's late-night adventure in pharmaceuticals was still sitting on the gravel road. The greenery seemed a little thicker than it had in the dark, but I chalked that up to imagination and poor eyesight.

"This is it," I announced unnecessarily, and ground to a halt. "Who's for a little grave robbing?"

"Not robbing," Ellie correct me primly. "We're just going to observe, and to pay our respects."

"Well, yes, that's what I meant..." I began, but she'd already marched off into the greenery, and we had no choice but to follow.

The graveyard, at least, seemed less impressive by day, and here and there shafts of sunlight managed to poke through to the forest floor. "Neat," said Harris, and I was inclined to agree. By night, the spot had a mystery and a power to it. By day it was ramshackle and quaint, still interesting but distinctly unmagical. "Neat" seemed to be about the best way to describe it, and I said so.

"You men. No sense of wonder," said Ellie, distinctly annoyed, and hoisted herself over the fence.

"Ellie, don't!" I called out. "This is private property. You shouldn't trespass."

She looked at me and laughed. "We're in the middle of the woods, silly. Who's going to see me? Besides, we're just here for a minute. I'll see what the stones say, and then we can leave and go back to," her voice shifted to a stentorian monotone, "building cross-departmental relationships by drinking heavily."

"Fine, whatever," I said, and turned away, irritated at myself. In truth, I really didn't want her going in there, but for reasons having nothing to do with trespassing. *How the hell am I supposed to impress her*, I asked myself, *if she keeps on taking all the chances*? And making the lame comment about property rights had, no doubt, made me look like even more of an idiot in her eyes. I kicked the fence angrily and spat down onto the dead leaves.

"Hey," Felix sidled up to me and gave me a disapproving look. "Don't kick the fence, dude. That's vandalism."

"Whatever." I shrugged and looked down at the fencepost I'd banged my foot against. It now leaned at a definite angle, and a surge of embarrassment shot through me. "Maybe the trees will come out and straighten the fence tonight," I said, a bit more harshly than was strictly necessary, and stared after Ellie as she picked her way among the brambles.

"If you'd seen what we'd seen, you wouldn't be making fun." The Cat's tone was dead serious, and I looked at him, surprised. Normally he couldn't keep a joke going for longer than your average commercial, but this time he seemed absolutely sincere. "You should probably tell Ellie to hold off on poking around in the woods tonight," he added, a trifle hesitantly. "She'll listen to you."

I laughed, softly. "She won't listen to me, even if I felt like telling her something like that, which I don't. You know how it is, man. You just get caught up in whatever she's doing, and go along for the ride." I gestured broadly, taking in the trees, the forest floor, and whatever else was in our vicinity. "Honestly, this is probably safer than hanging around our co-workers. At least the kudzu won't try to grope her, or throw up on her shoes."

He didn't laugh, instead poking me in the ribs with his elbow. "She will listen to you, man. She always does when it counts, whether you notice or not. And this counts. It really does." He paused and took a deep breath. "I've got a bad feeling, a real bad feeling about this place. If you care about her, keep her out of the woods at night."

I turned to face him. "She's a grown woman," I said softly. "She can make her own decisions."

"You can help her decide not to do something bone-stupid," he replied. "That means it's on you if you don't." And then he turned and walked away, heading for the road.

"Weird," I muttered, and turned back to watch Ellie. She was still in the graveyard, her jeans carefully dusted clean of rust and paint and whatever else she'd gotten on them while fence hopping. Now she squatted on her haunches in front of the biggest of the stones, her fingers tracing lines on its surface and her face screwed up in concentration.

I thought she looked adorable.

"What does it say?" I asked.

"It's hard to tell," she called back. From her tone of voice, she sounded like she was shouting, but it was almost hard to hear her. I looked around for evidence of wind that might drown her out, but there was none. Even the tops of the trees were perfectly still. The air was calm, and again, nothing living moved or betrayed its existence besides us.

"I think these are names," she said, and I leaned over the fence to hear her better. "It's the names of the family members. You can read the little flat stones—those are babies. No names. They died before they were christened. It's really sad."

"And the big ones?" I asked.

"The grownups, I guess." Her hand moved over the face of the tombstone, flat now against the dull red rock. "It's strange. The edges of the gravestones are sharp, like they're new, but the faces are all weathered and the writing's impossible to read. All I can really see are the dates. It's mostly 1820s to 1860s."

"So you were right," Harris interjected from across the graveyard. I shot him a look of annoyance, while Ellie grinned at him in delight. Needless to say, he kept his eyes on her.

"I was right!" she said, and bounced to her feet. "You know what I need?"

I sighed. "What?"

"Paper," she said firmly. "It's what you're supposed to do with tombstones. You put paper over them and do a rubbing," She rubbed her chin with her thumb. "I'll bet no one's ever done these before."

"Very few people wander into the South Carolina woods with an art studio in their back pocket," I responded, but she was already off, estimating the number of sheets she'd need, where she'd get the crayons to do the rubbings with, and so forth.

I looked down at my watch. It read 11:45, and I frowned. Surely we hadn't been there that long, and yet there the evidence was in blinking digital. "We should head back if we want lunch," I said, a little more softly. "If you want to get your tracing paper or whatever and get back here before it gets dark, the sooner we go, the better."

"Spoilsport," Ellie said, and stuck her tongue out at me. But then she smiled and hopped over the fence. "You're right, and I'm hungry." She hooked one arm through mine and the other through Harris' and grinned. "I feel like Dorothy," she said. "Let's go off to see the wizard."

"Marketing is doing the cooking," I warned. "It's not likely to be very magical."

"All the more reason to have fun now," she replied, and off we went.

S*omething* decidedly unmagical was waiting for us back at the bungalows, namely the looming figure of Hector. He was scowling when we trundled our way down the driveway, and kept scowling when we skidded to a halt in front of him.

"You missed the morning's programming," he said accusingly, waving a finger in my face for emphasis.

"Yes. We did." I said, as contrite as I could manage. "We went out for a walk after breakfast and... lost track of time."

"Yeah, yeah." He looked back over his shoulder at the main building. "Felix told me all about it when he got back an hour ago."

"An hour?" I was genuinely surprised. "I thought he was only five minutes ahead of us."

"Maybe on your planet," Hector said, and rubbed his eyes. "Look, there's been a change of plans. Due to discussions between us and the facility owners, we're going to leave first thing in the morning."

My "What happened?" was simultaneous with Ellie's "That's not fair" and Harris' knowing chuckle.

"Someone broke something, right?" he asked, and grinned wickedly.

"Something like that." Hector looked uncomfortable, and I got a sudden inkling that whatever had happened was extremely embarrassing for Hector personally. "There was what we will politely refer to as an *incident*, and they've asked us to leave. The details are unimportant. All you have to know is that we'll be going right after breakfast tomorrow." He paused and looked around, then continued in a lower voice, "I shouldn't tell you this, but they wanted us out immediately, but then we could have gotten most of our money back. Greedy bastards."

"That's just rude," Ellie opined, and stuck her hands on her hips like a '40s recruiting poster. "They can't do that, can they?"

"They can and they did, and we're not going to argue." Hector's tone was firm, and weary. "This weekend has not exactly been what you'd call a smashing success. Drinking, yes. Screwing, yes. Broken appliances in the bungalows, yes indeedy. Workshopping, not so much. And that's before we get into staff members taking off into the woods in the middle of the night to do God-knows-what in the local graveyards. So, here's what's going to happen. You three," and he pointed to each of us in turn, "are going to do the dishes from lunch, because not only did you skip out on morning programming, but you had a really stupid excuse for doing so. This afternoon, you get to go to the workshops and sit front and center, and if I don't see you there, I'll be telling your managers that you disobeyed a direct request from upper management. If that happens, it will be reflected in your performance and salary reviews. Tonight, you can do whatever the hell you want, but this afternoon your asses are mine. Or at least our workshop coordinator's. Am I understood?"

I could physically feel Ellie slumping next to me, and she dragged my heart down with her as she went. "Understood," I mumbled, and then put an arm around Ellie's shoulders. I turned to her. "Let's go get some lunch, OK? It'll make you feel better."

"In theory," Hector said, and walked off.

Night fell hard, and as it did, all hell broke loose. Word had gotten around the compound, reliable or not, that we were being forced to leave because an editor named John Blauser had smashed a lamp over someone's head in the complex's front office. Blauser denied the story vehemently, but it was too late; people had decided to stand up for his honor by being drunken louts. By 7:45, a hue and cry had gone up for us to get our money's worth out of being blacklisted, and the staff set to celebrating their last night out in the woods with a will. I counted at least two chairs in the bonfire down past the second row of bungalows, and one more that came flying through a second story window. Bottles were everywhere—full, empty, and in transit—and to the untrained ear, the sound of merriment would have been suspiciously similar to that of a riot.

"Let's go," Ellie said softly as we stood by the bonfire, our communal bag of marshmallows emphatically ignored by the other revelers.

I looked over at her. "Yeah, sure. Whatever. This is depressing the shit out of me."

"Me, too," and she headed for the main complex. "I almost wish we'd just gone back home this afternoon."

"Part of me does, too. This little bacchanal isn't going to help our company's reputation any. But we had to do those fucking workshops, and I don't feel like tackling these roads in the dark. Best to ignore the heathens," I said with an airy wave that took in our officemates, "and endure until morning."

"You're really not attractive when you swear," she said sweetly, and kept walking. "It's not you, and you sound silly doing it."

"Do I, now?" I walked a little faster, trying to catch up. "And what does make me attractive, if I may ask?"

"Being you," she said, and let it hang there for a moment. "I think that's attractive enough. Though I'm not sure about when you drink too much beer."

"The beer," I said firmly, "is an affectation, a feeble attempt to fit in with the rest of the company. I'll tell you a secret—I don't even really like the taste of it."

"I know," she said, and snickered, albeit nicely. "You make this really funny face every time you drink one."

I felt myself flushing bright red, and was thankful the bonfire light gave me camouflage. "I do? Damn. I'll have to stop that."

"Stop making the face?"

"Stop drinking beer." I stopped, and reached out for her hand. She let me, and turned to face me. Her face was very serious as she looked up at mine.

"Did you really mean that?" I asked. "That you find me attractive, I mean?"

A tiny smile quirked the corner of her mouth. "Do you always use pickup lines this smooth?"

"No, this is a special occasion." I blinked furiously, and thought very hard about what to say next. "What I mean to say is, well, I find you very attractive, too, and if you like me, maybe we could go someplace and just talk for a while. Get to know each other better." I caught myself before I said "and jump each others' bones," but I don't really think I needed to.

She smiled for real now, a very pretty smile. "That might be nice," she said softly. "But first, there's something I want to do with you."

"Yes?" Various visions floated through my head, most of them rated PG-13 and higher. "Name it."

She took a deep breath. "Let's go back to the graveyard tonight so I can do those rubbings. It will be so cool, and we can put them up in the office when we get back."

"I don't know," I said softly. "It sounded like Hector wasn't really up on the idea of us heading out there again, and besides, it might actually be dangerous."

"Oh, foo." Her face collapsed into a very pretty mask of disappointment. "I don't think it would be dangerous. I think it would be neat. And it's something that just you and I can do—something we can do together and share." The half-smile returned, and with it I knew I was doomed. "Besides," she added. "Wouldn't that make a great first date to tell people about?"

I thought about what I could possibly say to rebut that argument and realized that there were no arrows in my quiver. Say anything, and I risked losing her. Say nothing, and we'd take a short walk into woods that were noticeably free of any hostile critters, and get far enough away from the rest of the company that a little frisky business might be an option. I thought about Felix's warning for a moment, then dismissed it. Trees do not lean forward to eat pedestrians, even stoned ones, even in South Carolina.

I exhaled sharply. She stared up on me.

"Right. Let's go."

"Really?" Her face erupted into a smile and I felt ten feet tall. "You really want to go?"

"*Really* want to go is pushing it a bit," I confessed, "But I want to do it. Let's go get that paper you were talking about and do this thing before it gets too late."

"OK." She was positively chirping. "I got it and the crayons this afternoon, during the thing we did with the construction paper and the greeting cards we had to make for each other. Do you remember that?"

I did, and I shuddered at the memory. One of the interns had given me something that looked like an origami swan after a trip through a blender, and I was convinced she'd be peeking into my cube at least once a week from now on to make sure it occupied a place of honor. "Well, at least some good will come out of that exercise in time wasting."

"Yup. Lots of good." Very hesitantly, she pulled my face down to hers and kissed me. It was soft and it was quick, and the taste of her lips on mine was sweeter than I'd imagined it would be.

"Let's go," she whispered when we came up for air. "Let's hurry."

And then we were at the bungalow, and I held open the door with a smile that, I am quite certain, told Harris everything he needed to know.

He and Felix were inside, smoking gently and playing Uno. They both looked up at our entrance. Harris was pissed off, Felix disappointed.

"Just stopping in for a minute, guys," I said as Ellie vanished toward her room. "We're going out."

"Uh-huh," Harris said. "Where are you going?"

I shrugged. "She wants to do those rubbings. I can't stop her, so I might as well go along to make sure she doesn't get attacked by the local werewolves."

"Riiiiight." He turned back to his hand and studied it with calculated indifference. The Cat glowered at me and threw his cards down.

"I told you to stop her, man," he hissed, shaking his head. "Now you gotta protect her for real. Don't let anything get her out there, OK? Because it's your fault if they do."

"There is nothing out there to get her," I said through gritted teeth. "There aren't even any mosquitoes. She, and I, will be fine. We will go to the graveyard, she will do her rubbings, and we will come back here to join you gentlemen in your fine card game. This, I swear. Now will you please stop acting like a boy scout from a troop in Transylvania and leave me and her alone for a little while?"

"Her funeral, man," Felix grumbled, and turned away. Before I could call him on it, Ellie popped into the common area, a box of crayons under one arm and a poster tube under the other.

"I'm ready," she announced, and snuggled up close to me. She was smiling so hard she practically glowed. All coherent thought left my head and took a sharp turn south.

Harris turned a delicate shade of pink. The Cat just glowered down at his cards, squeezing them so hard they creased.

I walked into the bungalow's tiny excuse for a kitchen and grabbed the flashlight from where it rested, upright on the table. "Let's go," I said to her. "Let's go right now."

The walk to the graveyard was fast this time, far faster than it had any right to be. I carried the poster tube full of paper, and Ellie took care of the crayons. The entire way down was one long discussion over what color she should use. I favored copper, but she didn't want to use up all of the metallics "because they're people's favorites." I pointed out that if she didn't use them, someone else would, and besides, even with the lousy quarter the company had just had they could afford to spot us a few new boxes of crayons. She didn't reply to that directly, but gave a thoughtful hum and walked—no, skipped, really—on.

Only twice did I look away from her as we made our way into the night. Once, I looked down to make sure that my shoes were in fact tied, because the last thing I wanted to do was trip in front of Ellie and make myself look like a fool. The other time, I looked up, and reassured myself that the sky and stars were still there.

They were.

Feeling much more secure about my place in the grand scheme of things, I put my eyes back on Ellie and followed her on into the night.

The stretch of road that ran past the gravesite was ridiculously easy to find. The half-curtain of kudzu that had been there in the morning was entirely gone, leaving a gaping, not entirely inviting gap in the greenery.

"We must have knocked it down on the way out," Ellie said, a trifle hesitantly, and I nodded slightly. To cover my discomfort, I looked around for any fronds or leaves on the ground, but there weren't any. Apparently the voracious kudzu had already re-integrated its fallen manifestations, or some animal had come along and eaten it.

The thought that it had deliberately gotten out of our way didn't linger in my mind for more than a minute and a half, I swear. Honest.

"Shall we?" she asked, and I bowed.

"Allow me to go first. It might be dangerous."

She giggled. "And you have the flashlight."

"That I do," I said ruefully. "So much for trying to impress you."

"You don't have to impress me, silly. Now let's go."

Her tone brooked no argument, so I didn't argue. I just ducked under the lowest hanging of the tree branches and stepped into the woods, and listened, like Orpheus, for the sound of her following.

The forest was different tonight. I could sense that immediately. Where the night before, everything had been silent as a newborn's nursery, tonight the trees were alive with sound. There were no animal noises, though—none of the cicada and cricket songs that I had heard back among the bungalows, no night bird calls or frog song or bat chirps tickling the upper edge of hearing. It just sounded leafy, for lack of a better term; wood creaking and branches snapping and leaves rustling against each other in the breeze.

There hadn't been a breeze when we'd walked down, I remembered. Just hot, sticky southern air.

It means nothing, I told myself. *Branches move all the time. You're letting Felix get to you. There's got to be a breeze higher up, away from the road.* And to prove the point to myself, I pointed the flashlight straight up for a moment, and illuminated the underside of the leaves on high.

They were, I saw as a cold feeling settled into my stomach, perfectly still.

"Ellie?" I ventured, hesitantly.

"Don't tell me you're getting scared!" she taunted from behind me, and then hurried past. I cursed, under my breath so she wouldn't hear, and went after her. She heard my footsteps in the leaves, laughed, and ran faster. I tripped over a hidden tree root but held onto the flashlight, cursed again, got to my feet, and kept running. *Keep the flashlight on her,* something told me. *Keep her in the light.* And so I did, even when that meant running my shins into tree stumps and my legs into thorns. I ran as fast as I dared, keeping her just in sight, and wondered how fucking far it was to the graveyard because it hadn't been one tenth this long in the morning. Vines I hadn't seen scored my face, patches in the dry ground suddenly became muddy and treacherous, and every step seemed to be uphill. Ellie, for her part, ran on as I fell further and further behind her.

And then suddenly, she was there at the fence, and I pulled up, puffing, ten seconds after she did.

"Slowpoke," she said, and pointed to the gate. "See?"

The gate was open. The graveyard itself was utterly bereft of weeds, and there was a note on yellow paper, taped to one of the fence posts.

"What does it say?" I asked, and immediately felt like an idiot.

"I don't know," she replied. "I'll read it and find out."

She picked it up, and I took the flashlight and held it over her shoulder so she could read. The note was folded over a few times with great precision, but when she'd finished opening it up there were only a few words there, hand-written in a rough blocky print.

"Sorry the place is such a mess," it said. "If I'd known folks were going to be visiting family, I would have cleaned it up. Stay as long as you want." There was no signature.

"Well, that's very nice," Ellie said, and tucked the note in her pocket. "And you were so worried about trespassing."

"I don't know," I said. "Something about that note just doesn't feel right."

"You're being paranoid," she said firmly.

"Probably," I admitted. "But could I see the note anyway? Just in case?"

"Fine." She dug into her pocket and handed it over, wordless irritation emanating from her in all directions.

I cringed, but took the note. It seemed straightforward enough, but something still nagged at me. I stared at the yellow paper, trying to decipher hidden meaning in the words, when suddenly it hit me.

The paper itself was the problem. It felt rough underneath my fingers, and under the flashlight it seemed weathered and old. Whoever had cleaned out the graveyard had left their note on a scrap that seemed like it had been stuck in a bush for years, and that, I thought, was odd.

"Well?"

I started to open my mouth to explain what I'd discovered, but decided against it. What could I say? "Hey, the paper the note is on is old?" It hardly seemed enough to dissuade her. Instead, I just gestured with the flashlight to the open gate, and tucked the note away. She took the hint and walked into the graveyard. I followed, and when she silently extended her hand for the poster tube, I handed it over.

That's when I got the evening's second shock, third if you counted Ellie kissing me. The soil inside hadn't been weeded, I now saw. Instead, it had been ravaged. Someone had come through and yanked out every bit of plant life. Every bramble, every weed, every blade of grass—gone. Nothing had been merely trimmed and let off with a warning. It had all been pulled out by the roots, leaving nothing but soil dark with rotted leaf mulch and gaping holes where weeds and creepers used to be.

Ellie walked on. She didn't seem to have noticed any of this. I got the sense that she didn't want to.

Still, the disquiet wouldn't leave me alone. As Ellie looked at stones, I stared down at the soil until she finally caught me doing it.

"Would you cut that out?" she asked. "It's distracting. We're not here for the dirt, you know."

"Sorry," I apologized. "I was just wondering who left the note. I mean, no one lives here, so they couldn't have seen us. No one knew that this was where we'd been until Felix—excuse me, The Cat—shot his mouth off today. It's just weird, that's all."

"You worry too much," she said, as she held up crayon after crayon in the flashlight beam. "Someone probably saw us go in, saw the junk the guys left on the road, or came to visit the graveyard and saw our footprints." She pulled something reddish out and matched it to a parchment-colored piece of paper. "There, I think. That's it."

I gave a half-hearted nod. "If you say so. I just don't know who lives out here. We never heard any cars go past on the road while we were in here."

"Maybe they drove slowly. You know how weird the sound out here is. Now hush, and give me more light." She put the paper to the stone and began working. I stood there, occasionally adjusting the angle of the light as she requested it, and watched her work. Part of me wondered if our trespassing had been what had really gotten the company kicked out of the resort. If that were the case, though, they wouldn't have weeded and left a note. I pondered that for a minute, and then the rest of me told me to shut up and watch Ellie, because she was damned cute and if I held the light at just the right angle I could see a little further down her shirt than an entirely honorable man ought to.

"Done," she finally said, holding the rubbing up to the light. I peered in at it, but even as I looked she rolled it up and moved on to the next stone. I checked the flashlight, which still seemed to be going strong, and patted my pocket for the emergency backup: a lighter. It wasn't my first choice for a method of lighting our way in the woods, but things seemed reasonably green fireproof and besides, for all I knew we were a hundred miles from the nearest convenience store with a Duracell display. The last thing I wanted was to run out of light out here. It would be a long, long walk back in the dark.

Thinking about it made me nervous, so I decided to see if Ellie could be hurried a little bit. "How's it going?" I asked.

"Fine," she replied distractedly. "You could do one, too, if you wanted to."

"I wouldn't be able to hold the flashlight then," I replied sensibly.

"I'll hold it and you can do one when I'm done with this stone," she said, and her tone informed me that yes, I was going to be doing exactly as she had described.

"All right," I responded. "But only if I can use the copper crayon."

"Okay," she said, and then put her head down and went back to work.

An hour, or maybe five minutes later, she announced, "Done!"

"Does that mean we can go back now?" I asked.

"No, silly. It means it's your turn. If you don't do one, we can hardly say we did this together."

"I feel I've shed a certain light on the proceedings," I half-protested.

"Very funny." She stood, handed me a piece of paper, and extended her empty hand. "Give me the flashlight."

"Fine, fine," I said. With one hand I took the paper, and with the other I gave her the flashlight. The beam was giving the faintest hints of dimming, or so my nervous hindbrain informed me, so I hurriedly grabbed a crayon that looked right out of the box and looked at my choice of workspaces. "Got any suggestions?"

"That one," she said, and pointed with the light to one at the end of a row. It was small and squat, but even from here looked to have been fairly intricately carved at one point. "Do that one."

"Works for me," I said, and set myself down by it to go to work.

The procedure for doing that sort of rubbing is pretty simple. You take the paper, tape it up so it holds still, then rub the side of the crayon along it so the carving underneath manifests itself in beeswax and coloring. We didn't have any tape, so instead I got to hold the paper up with one hand, thankful there was no wind, and scribble with the other.

And even as I did that, I heard the wind up there among the leaves, and did my damndest to ignore it. Behind me, Ellie held the flashlight, making suggestions as I went along, and I tried hard not to think about The Cat's warning.

By the time I was done, the flashlight had dimmed visibly, and, judging by the degree of recurring droopiness in the beam's position, Ellie's wrists had gotten tired. "I think we're done here," I said gently. "Let's go and look at these things in the light, to see what we've got." Carefully, I rolled up my rubbing and stuck it in the poster tube, then turned back to Ellie to show her I was ready to go.

She stood there, both hands clutching the dying light and pointing it straight up. I could see that she was shivering, even in the muggy heat of the forest, and her eyes were held tightly shut. "Could you tell me..." She started in a high, shrill voice, and then stopped. She took a deep breath, swallowed, and tried again. "Could you tell me what you see behind me? Please?" She took another deep breath that was almost a sob, and whispered, "I thought I heard something."

"Something?" I said, and looked up.

"Something," she affirmed, and now she was crying for real, the flashlight shaking in her grip. "*Something called my name.*"

She stood at the edge of the graveyard, maybe a foot and a half from the fence. Her feet were carefully positioned on the neutral ground between two graves, so close together that she teetered as if she stood on a balance beam. Behind her, there should only have been the fence, and then a space of brush and undergrowth leading to the road. That's what had been there yesterday, that's what had been there that morning, that's what had been there when we'd been invited in among the tombstones.

But now the trees were there. Cloaked in green, reaching forward for her, wind-whispering something that might have been her name even as the branches creaked down and the boughs stretched out.

"Ellie," I said very calmly, "Why don't you take a step toward me? There's nothing to worry about. Just come on over here and give me the flashlight, OK?"

"OK," she said, and took a step. Behind her, a sheet of vines dropped to the ground with a hiss. Where the leaves hit the ground, they crept forward, toward Ellie.

She took another step, and another, and I walked towards her with the poster tube held up like I imagined a broadsword was supposed to be.

"What's behind me?" she asked, almost too softly to be heard.

"Nothing that's not supposed to be," I told her, and hated myself for the lie. "Nothing called your name."

And this wasn't a lie, because I could hear the trees now, hear the nonexistent wind moving the kudzu leaf tongues, and I knew what they were saying. They might have called Ellie once, but they weren't calling her name any more.

They were calling mine.

"We're going to go back now, Ellie," I said very loudly as I took the flashlight from her hands. "We're going to leave the crayons here as a present for the nice man who cleaned up the graveyard, and we're going to go back. I'll hold the flashlight and the rubbings. All you have to do is hold onto me. Do you think you can do that?"

She nodded, tears streaking her face. Her eyes were still closed, and her hands reached out and flattened themselves against my chest. "I think that's a very good idea," she said, and pulled herself close.

"That's good, stay close to me," I heard myself saying, all the while trying to figure out how the hell I was going to get us out of this. The carpet of vines had inched forward into the graveyard proper, snaking between the fence posts in places and yanking them out of the soil in others. All through the forest, I could hear the sounds they were making as the things that had once been trees pulled themselves closer to where we stood. There was no time, I knew that now. The longer we delayed, the tighter the green cordon would be pulled around us, and all I had was a dying flashlight and a three-foot length of cardboard.

And Ellie, whom I'd promised Felix I would keep safe.

"All right, Ellie," I said, keeping my voice as calm as I could. "I need you to do something else for me, right now."

"What?"

"I need you to open your eyes and not scream, all right?"

She managed most of it, the scream coming out as a sort of choking sound. I didn't blame her. I wanted to scream myself, but I knew that if I did, I would pretty much just get caught up in the screaming, at least until I got caught up in something worse and leafier.

I wrapped my left arm around her and pulled Ellie with me toward the gate. By some miracle, it was still unblocked, though the place where Ellie had been standing a minute before was already underneath the leaves. They were growing fast, snaking around the

38

tombstones, and probing in all directions. A half-dozen tendrils were already growing toward us, moving fast. Behind them, the things that had once been trees leaned in closer. Their voices were louder now. They didn't care who heard them.

We got through the gate and I pulled Ellie to the left. "We're going to have to run now," I said, but she was way ahead of me, sprinting back toward the way we'd come. I felt her slip out from under my arm and started pounding after her, the flashlight's beam fading to a dull yellow and barely keeping her in view. I could half-see, half-hear the terrain in front of us; I didn't dare look behind. Branches wrapped in leafy armor came crashing down, impaling the earth and narrowly missing Ellie. Curtains of vines threw themselves in front of her, reaching out to entangle, and she hurled herself past them.

I didn't have time for that, knew she'd slip out of the light if I dared dodge and weave, and so I trusted to brute strength and just charged straight through. Where I pushed through the vines, they grasped at me, tearing and clinging. Where they touched me, I could feel them probing and pushing, trying to get under the skin. They wanted me, I suddenly understood, to run me through and fill me up and turn me into another one of those figures in the wood.

That would be the beginning, at least. Because the vines here didn't want to stay in the woods, didn't want to just strangle trees and cover shrubs any more. They wanted something more challenging, something more *alive*. They wanted me to walk out in the morning with vines trailing out of my feet and curling out of my eyes, and to pass that contagion on to everyone else.

I thought about what might have tended the graves so very carefully, and wondered if right now that green figure was shambling after me, vines spilling out of his mouth and leaves covering his eyes.

I thought about it catching up to Ellie, and I ran faster.

That's when a tree stump came up out of the ground and hit me.

It had been there before. I'm sure I saw it on the way in. But then it had been a little thing, maybe six inches above the leaves. Now it was something more, wrapped in kudzu and punching its way upward even as I stepped over it. It slammed into my balls and I went over, howling. The flashlight flew out of my fingers, smashed into a tree, and went out. I hit the ground with my shoulder, rolled, and tried to stagger to my feet. The poster tube, of course, I'd managed to hang on to, and I leaned on it now like a cane. "Ellie!" I called. "Ellie!"

"I'm here!" she replied, faintly, far too faintly. "I can see the road!"

"Keep going!" I told her, even as I heard the vines slithering around my feet. "Don't worry about me! Go!"

The sound of her footsteps stopped. "Are you sure?"

"Yes!" My voice broke, and I prayed she wouldn't ask me again. I wasn't sure how I'd answer if she did.

She didn't respond, which I took as a good sign. Faintly, I heard her footsteps, and then they were gone.

That left me alone, in the dark, and all I had to do was concentrate on getting myself out of there. The flashlight was gone, and I was sure I'd heard the bulb shatter when it hit. There was no sense looking for it, not when the tree-things were lurching and roaring closer in the dark.

I started walking, half-bent over in pain, toward the direction from which I'd last heard Ellie's voice. I leaned on the poster tube as much as I dared, staggering on while I went through my pockets looking for the lighter. It took a couple of tries to find it, more time than I liked. With shaking fingers I pulled it out and tried to flick it.

No dice.

Panicking, I dropped the tube with the rubbings and grabbed the lighter with both hands, trying desperately to keep my grip from shaking.

In the near dark, tree limbs groaned with the effort of reaching out for me.

"Come on," I implored the lighter, and flicked it with trembling fingers. I caught a whiff of lighter fluid, but no spark.

Something moved underneath the leaves by my feet, slithering whip-fast and closer.

"Come on!" I flicked it again, praying under my breath.

It flared to life, a tiny beacon in the middle of a very dark place. "Thank you God, " I breathed, and looked around.

The vines had me. A solid wall of greenery hemmed me in. Every direction was blocked off. Even if I had known where to run, I wouldn't have gotten far before the kudzu would have caught me like a fly. I was trapped.

I held up the lighter. Trapped, yes, but with fire.

"Back off," I said, and spun in a slow circle. "You heard me, back off, or I'll burn you all down!" An empty threat, I knew, but it was the only card I had to play. I stared into the flame of the lighter, willing it to get bigger. It didn't listen.

There was a dry rattle of leaves, and a single vine snaked its way toward me from a low-hanging branch. Somehow I grabbed it, though it twisted like a snake, and held the lighter to it.

It didn't burn, but it smoked, and that was enough. It jerked itself out of my grasp in a manner of seconds.

A heartbeat after that, the trees were moving, creating a space for me. Branches jerked themselves away with a groan. Vines hissed on dry leaves as they drew back into the dark. The road beckoned, shockingly close.

"Oh yeah," I said, backing away quickly lest the forest change its mind. "I've got this, and there's more where it came from. Don't forget it, or I'll be back with aerosol cans and friends." I was hysterical now, laughing and crying and taunting the trees, and sure that there was one last trick they'd play on me before I reached the road.

I was wrong. There was none, no last-ditch attempt to snag me around the ankles or by the throat. I just passed through that last curtain of leaves, and suddenly there was freedom right in front of me. Three steps, and I was in the road. I collapsed onto the gravel, bleeding from a dozen different places, and the lighter went out. I let it stay out and slowly picked myself up. Of Ellie, there was no sign.

"Must have kept running, like I told her," I told myself, and started limping back toward the resort. "She must have."

At the time, I even believed it.

Ellie's door was closed when I got back to the bungalow, and I didn't feel inclined to barge on in. Any thoughts of romance were long gone, replaced by bone weariness and pain. Bloody and dirty, I just collapsed on the couch. There was enough time to kick one shoe off before sleep claimed me, and I welcomed it when it did.

Harris woke me up what felt like five minutes later.

"Where is she, man? *Where is she?*"

I blinked and stared blearily up at him. "What?"

"Ellie!" His voice was frantic with worry. "Where is she?"

"She came home before I did. I told her to run, she ran, and... what?" I sat bolt upright. "She's not back?"

"No, she's not." He stood, arms crossed on his chest. Behind him, Felix was pulling on shoes. "You came in around five. She never did."

"But she left the woods before I did!" I exclaimed. "When the trees came for us, I got her out. I swear, I got her out!"

Felix shot me a look of pure disgust. "Sure you did," he said, and then to Harris, "Let's go."

"Wait." I swung my legs off the couch. "I'm coming with you."

"No, you're not," Harris replied. "You've done enough, thanks."

"Please," I said. "I have to. I need to find out that she's all right."

They looked at each other. "Fine," Harris said, finally. "Fuckup," said Felix at the same time.

We went in silence, neither of them willing to look at me. I limped along as best I could, but a few hours' sleep had made me realize how badly I'd been pummeled the night before. Every muscle was stiff, a hundred cuts burned where the kudzu had slashed me, and my balls ached so badly that I was afraid to contemplate the shape they were in.

Ahead of me, Harris and The Cat stopped. I limped up to where they stood, stared, and blinked back tears.

This was the place. I could see bloodstains, my bloodstains in the road. I could see the old evidence of Harris and The Cat sitting in the gravel and lighting up. I could see footprints new and old, and I could see a roughly me-sized hole in the curtain of kudzu that hid the undergrowth from the road.

But I couldn't find any evidence that Ellie had made it out last night.

"She said she could see the road," I said softly. "She said she was going to make it. I told her to leave me behind."

Felix turned and looked at me. He didn't say anything. He didn't have to.

Deep down, I knew. It wasn't the fire that had gotten me out. It was the fact that they already had Ellie.

"Are we going in?" I asked, afraid of the answer.

"No," said Harris. "The cops might be, though, so we're not going to mess anything up in there. Besides, you and I both know what sort of things happen here. There's not going to be anything to see. We won't find her."

As he spoke, the hole in the greenery started knitting itself back up. Felix saw this, shook his head and turned to go. He and Harris saw the kudzu, and they knew they wouldn't see anything more.

But I did. I saw something else, something the green wanted to show me.

I saw Ellie.

She was back there in the woods, leaves barely covering her soft white skin. She was naked now, naked except for the vines that had wrapped themselves around her waist and twined themselves in her hair. Her eyes were open, and I could tell she could see me just as I saw her. In her left hand was the poster tube, shot through now with leafy strands of kudzu. She held it up to me so I could see she had it, and as she did, the curtain widened again.

Harris and Felix didn't see any of it. They had already turned away.

I saw, though. I saw her lips move, impossibly far off in the forest, as she spoke to me.

I heard her, too, Ellie's voice whispered to me by a thousand leaves.

She said one word.

Together.

I felt myself blinking back tears. She smiled.

"Together soon enough," I told her, and walked away.

About the Author

Formerly a game developer for White Wolf, Richard Dansky has published four novels, including the Trilogy of the Second Age. His short fiction has been published in A Fistful o' Dead Guys, Stillwaters Journal, and Dark Tyrants, and will appear this year in Crypto-Critters and Quietus magazine. He has written, designed, or otherwise contributed to over 120 role-playing game books, and has also written for, among others, Lovecraft Studies, InQuest, PC Power, and Yes! The Magazine of Positive Futures.

Currently, Richard is the Manager of Design for Red Storm Entertainment, in Morrisville, North Carolina. He's designed or otherwise contributed to numerous titles, including Ghost Recon: Island Thunder, Rainbow Six: Raven Shield, and The Sum of All Fears.

He lives in Durham, North Carolina with his fiancée Melinda Thielbar and their two inevitable cats.

About the Cover Artist

For over ten years, Angi Shearstone has been designing, illustrating, and otherwise creating for publishers, and ad agencies, electronics, packaging, and insurance companies, including Mercer Mayer Productions, CheckerBee Publishing and MassMutual Life Insurance. Her watercolors have earned national recognition in the Society of Illustrators Scholarship Competition (1990, 1991), and her recent exploration into Chinese painting and Sumi-e is attracting increasing attention from galleries and private collectors. She recently co-designed and contributed to *Myths and Monsters*, a self-published anthology of Savannah-based comic creators.

Since completing her MFA in Sequential Art, Angi has returned to her graphic design and illustration business with the intention of expanding further into comic books and publishing.

She recently relocated to Durham, NC, along with two forgiving cats and an awful lot of art supplies. For more information, please see www.angishearstone.com.

Yard Dog Press Titles as Of This Print Date

A Bubba in Time Saves None, Edited by Selina Rosen
A Man, A Plan, (yet lacking) A Canal, Panama, Linda Donahue
Adventures of the Irish Ninja, Selina Rosen
The Alamo and Zombies, Jean Stuntz
All the Marbles, Dusty Rainbolt
Almost Human, Gary Moreau
Ancient Enemy, Lee Killough
Angels of Mercy, Laura J. Underwood
Another Breath, Gary Moreau
The Anthology from Hell: Humorous Tales From WAY Down Under, Edited by
     Julia S. Mandala
Ard Magister, Laura J. Underwood
Assassins Inc., Phillip Drayer Duncan
Assassins Incorporated: Rehired, Phillip Drayer Duncan
Bad City, Selina Rosen & Laura J. Underwood
Bad Lands, Selina Rosen & Laura J. Underwood
Black Rage, Selina Rosen
Blackrose Avenue, Mark Shepherd
The Boat Man, Selina Rosen
Bobby's Troll, John Lance
Bride of Tranquility, Tracy S. Morris
Bruce and Roxanne from Start to Finnish, Rie Sheridan Rose
The Bubba Chronicles, Selina Rosen
Bubba Fables, Sue P. Sinor
Bubbas Of the Apocalypse, Edited by Selina Rosen
The Burden of the Crown (#3 in the Sword Masters Series), Selina Rosen
Chains of Freedom, Selina Rosen
Chains of Destruction, Selina Rosen
Chains of Redemption, Selina Rosen
Checking On Culture, Lee Killough
Chronicles of the Last War, Laura J. Underwood
Dadgum Martians Invade the Lucky Nickel Saloon, Ken Rand
Dark and Stormy Nights, Bradley H. Sinor
Deja Doo, Edited by Selina Rosen
Dracula's Lawyer, Julia S. Mandala
Dragon's Tongue, Laura J. Underwood
Escape Velocities, Brian A. Hopkins
The Essence of Stone, Beverly A. Hale
Fairy BrewHaHa at the Lucky Nickel Saloon, Ken Rand
The Fantastikon: Tales of Wonder, Robin Wayne Bailey
Fire & Ice, Selina Rosen
Flush Fiction, Volume I: Stories To Be Read In One Sitting, Edited by Selina Rosen
Flush Fiction, Volume II: Twenty Years of Letting it Go!, Edited by Selina Rosen

Strange Robby, Selina Rosen
Sword Masters (#1 in the Sword Masters Series), Selina Rosen
Tales from Keltora, Laura J. Underwood
Tales of the Lucky Nickel Saloon, Second Ave., Laramie, Wyoming, U S of A, Ken Rand
Tarbox Station, Rhonda Eudaly
The Territories (#5 in the Sword Masters Series),, Selina Rosen
Texistani: Indo-Pak Food from a Texas Kitchen, Beverly A. Hale
That's All Folks, J. F. Gonzalez
Through Wyoming Eyes, Ken Rand
Tranquility, Tracy Morris
Turn Left to Tomorrow, Robin Wayne Bailey
The Twins (#4 in the Sword Masters Series),, Selina Rosen
The Undead At My Head, Ethan Nahté
Villains in Training, Julia S. Mandala and Linda L. Donahue
Wandering Lark, Laura J. Underwood
Weirdough, Inc., Selina Rosen and Sherri Dean
Wings of Morning, Katharine Eliska Kimbriel
Zombies in Oz and Other Undead Musings, Robin Wayne Bailey

Fantasy Writers Asylum (A YDP Imprint):

Blood Songs, Julia Mandala
Chaos Heir: Beholden A. D. Guzman
Death's Paladin Christopher Donahue
Gateway to Corimar, Julia Mandala & Linda L. Donahue
Spirit Poles, Julia Mandala & Linda L. Donahue
Tale of the Black Heart, Linda L. Donahue
Traitor's Gate, Linda L. Donahue & Julia Mandala

Double Dog (A YDP Imprint):

#1:
Of Stars & Shadows, Mark W. Tiedemann
This Instance of Me, Jeffrey Turner

#3:
Home Is the Hunter, James K. Burk
Farstep Station, Lazette Gifford

#4:
Sabre Dance, Melanie Fletcher
The Lunari Mask, Laura J. Underwood

#5:
House of Doors, Julia Mandala
Jaguar Moon, Linda A. Donahue

Just Cause (A YDP Imprint):